Trick or Treat

SPOOKY POEMS CHOSEN BY
PAUL COOKSON

ILLUSTRATED
BY DAVID PARKINS

MACMILLAN CHILDREN'S BOOKS

Dedicated to John Foster, the
Uncle Remus of children's poetry –
a poetical trickster who's always a treat

First published 2005
by Macmillan Children's Books
a division of Macmillan Publishers Limited
20 New Wharf Road, London N1 9RR
Basingstoke and Oxford
www.panmacmillan.com

Associated companies throughout the world

ISBN 0 330 42630 3

3 5 7 9 8 6 4 2

A CIP catalogue record for this book is available from the British Library.

Printed by Mackays of Chatham plc, Chatham, Kent.

CONTENTS

Trick or Treat

Trick or treat, trick or treat
Pumpkins light up every street
Trick or treat, trick or treat
Witches watch and gremlins greet
Trick or treat, trick or treat
Skeletons and vampires meet
Trick or treat, trick or treat

Halloween, Halloween
Ghosts and ghouls glowing green
Halloween, Halloween
Werewolves, hairy, scary, mean
Halloween, Halloween
Mummies lurch and monsters lean
Hallo Hallo Halloween.

Paul Cookson

Halloween Pie

What do you put into Halloween pie?
A bat's leather wing, a chameleon's eye;
A crystal of frost and a red lick of fire,
Midnight's last chime and a scream rising higher;
A bright drop of blood and a shadowy shape
Of something that passes, leaving all mouths agape;

A pinch of excitement, a frisson of fear,
A sigh of relief and a loud rousing cheer
For the hero who rescues the lonely and lost,
Defeating the monster who learns to his cost
That whatever is bad fights what is noble and good –
And if you've never thought that, then maybe you
    should!

For that's what you put into Halloween pie,
Along with the dark of a cold autumn sky;
A little of this and a little of that,
And the green moonstone eyes of an old witch's cat . . .
Eat a piece and you'll find a fine lesson's been taught –
Cut a slice and take home some grim food for
    thought.

Stephen Bowkett

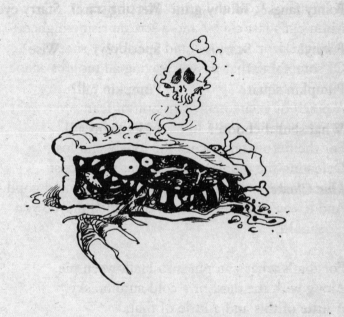

Decisions, Decisions

Pumpkin fat?   Pumpkin thin?

Pointy fangs? Toothy grin? Piercing stare? Starry eyes?

Funny?   Scary?   Spooky?   Wise?

Pumpkin squat?   Pumpkin tall?

What shall I choose?   I like them all!

Jane Clarke

Some Halloween Traditions That Didn't Catch On

Bobbing for pumpkins
Bobbing for peas
Bobbing for bricks
Bobbing for cheese

Treacle coffee, treacle tofu
Treacle potatoes, treacle soup
Treacle hot dogs, treacle chestnuts
Treacle apples, treacle fruit

Carving lanterns from parsnips
Carving lanterns from baked beans
Carving lanterns from cardboard boxes
Carving lanterns from ice cream

Toffee covered pork pies
Toffee covered kippers
Toffee covered cabbage
Toffee covered slippers

Shouting Trick or Feet!
Shouting Brick or Meat!
Shouting Stick or Tree!
Shouting Toilet Seat!

Paul Cookson and David Harmer

Nothing That Lives Is Ever Lost

Nothing that lives is ever lost.
Nor does it become a thing
So ordinary as a ghost.

But quietly, mysteriously
as silent snowfalls in the blue of night,
Life leaves
To live again inside God's shining light.

And when All Hallows comes
We celebrate this holiness, this heaven –
Filled with bright singing
Luminous as flames.

Nothing that lives is ever lost
And in his brightness
God knows all our names.

Jan Dean

Skeletons in Wellingtons

Skeletons in Wellingtons
went jangling down the street,
rapping doors and cackling,
yelling, 'Trick or treat?'

Skeletons in Wellingtons!
Folk couldn't believe their eyes
Skeletons in Wellingtons!
What a horrible surprise.

Skeletons in Wellingtons
played tricks and shouted, 'Boo!'
Doors were slammed and curtains pulled
as the skeletons marched through.

Then the Skeletons in Wellingtons
met a girl of eight years old.
'Why are you wearing Wellingtons?'
she asked. 'Our feet get cold,'

cried the Skeletons in Wellingtons,
'The wind is something cruel,
whistling through our foot bones.
Don't they teach you that at school?'

Then the Skeletons in Wellingtons
departed with a wave
and left their Wellies neatly parked
at dawn, upon their graves.

Marian Swinger

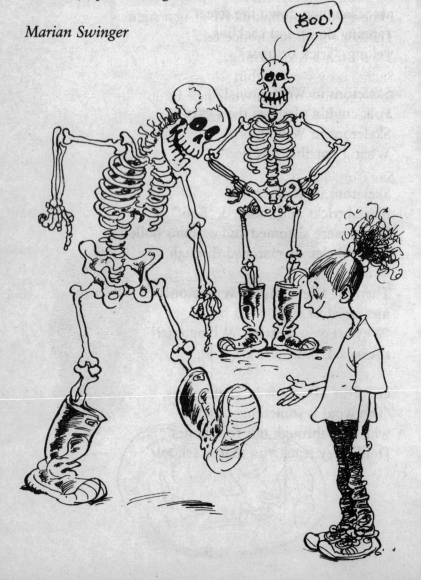

Pumpkin Love Song

When you appeared in the window
Of number thirty-three
I knew it was pumpkin love at first sight
Though you didn't notice me.
Then I felt a fire burning,
Such a cosy glow within –
Imagine my joy when your face lit up
As you fell for my jagged grin!

Sue Cowling

The Hour When the Witches Fly

When the night is as cold as stone,
When lightning severs the sky,
When your blood is chilled to the bone,
That's the hour when the witches fly.

When the night owl swoops for the kill,
When there's death in the fox's eye,
When the snake is coiled and still,
That's the hour when the witches fly.

When the nightmares scream in your head,
When you hear a strangled cry,
When you startle awake in your bed,
That's the hour when the witches fly.

When the sweat collects on your brow,
When the minutes tick slowly by,
When you wish it was then not now,
That's the hour when the witches fly.

John Foster

If I'm Seen on Halloween, Watch Out!

It's rubbish now at Halloween
Look out there, see what I mean?

Crowds of kids, what a sight
I'm the ghost, tonight's my night.

Silly costumes, witches' hats
Plastic spiders, rubber bats

No room to breathe because of you
Not that breathing's what I do.

I just can't scare you, I'm a joke
Not a ghastly, ghostly bloke.

When I go BOO to drive you mad
You simply think I'm someone's dad.

Pull out my eyes to make you sick
You all shout 'What a trick!'

I float two metres off the floor
You just yell 'Give us more!'

I groan and moan, shake my chain
You all cry 'Again, again!'

It's not fair, I just can't win
I think I might as well join in.

I pretend to trick or treat
You might see me on your street.

But when I give your door a knock
You're going to get a real shock.

You see, my friends, I'm for real
Full of scary spook appeal.

A waking nightmare, then you'll see
What happens when you mess with me.

David Harmer

After You, Bryony

I don't mind
apple bobbing
after Bryony
or Scott,
but after Nik
I'd rather not
(she's got a cold,
might leave some snot).

Mike Johnson

The Broomstick That Wouldn't Fly!

My brother believes everything
He's astonishingly green
He thinks that all the ghosts and ghouls
Are real on Halloween!

He believes in thirsty vampires
He believes in elves and sprites
He believes that werewolves come alive
When the moon is full at night!

But now he's in the hospital
With a painful broken leg
He got while trying to fly a broom
From the top of Grandad's shed!

We heard him land with quite a crash
We heard him scream and cry
He doesn't now believe
That broomsticks have the power to fly!

Ian Bland

Halloween Treat

'It's dark.'
'Eyeballs,
I can feel eyeballs!'
'It's not eyeballs.'
'Too small.'
'Eyeballs squidge.'
'Eyeballs pop!'
'They're grapes!'
'They're great?'
'GRAPES – you EAT!'
'Ohwww – cheat!'

'What's this?'
'Snot!'
'It's true – feel it, see?'
'It is sticky.'
'Ughh, snot!'
'It's not snot.'
'Snot's slidy.'
'It's not!'
'It TIZZ!'
'It's porridge.'
'Ohwww – swizz!'

'Feel these – '
'Toenails!'
'They are, you know!'
'What's it really?'
'I dunno . . .'
'Put the light on!'
'What's the trick?'

'Toenails!'
'REALLY toenails!'
'Yuk!'
'That's SICK!'

Liz Brownlee

Pumpkin Pie

(A telestich*)

More pumpkin pie? I've had enough
For breakfast, lunch and afternoon tea.
I've had so much I don't feel well.
I'm sure I'll have a dizzy spell.
My body's cold, a chill igloo.
I must have drunk a poisoned brew
Made quickly on a broomstick ride
By some weird witch – a devil's bride.
I won't eat pumpkin pie again!

John Kitching

*A telestich is a poem in which the last letter of each line spells
out a word.

22

A Bedtime Prayer for Halloween

Protect me from vampires
Protect me from ghouls
Protect me from phantoms
And howling werewolves
Protect me from witches
Protect me from ghosts
Protect me from my brother Sid
I fear him the most.

Richard Caley

A Wicked Taste

At Halloween our dinner ladies
cooked up a witches' brew,
full of nasty frogs' legs
and bits of spiders too.

They were only joking,
though we were not too sure,
but still we ate it up
and even asked for more!

It was really tasty
in a rotten sort of way,
in fact, give us witches' brew
instead of school dinners any day!

Andrew Collett

Purrfect Accessories

Chloe brought Tigger,
Sunita brought Scruff,
Jenny brought Sooty,
Elena brought Fluff.

Dara brought Gnasher,
Latoya brought Mouse,
Katie brought one that she
Found near her house.

I brought Napoleon,
Rachel brought Ben,
Laura brought Whiskers.
I think that made ten.

It was quite chaotic
I'd have to agree
But Miss overreacted,
Definitely.

She screamed and she hollered
And said they must go
Or she'd cancel the party
But we said, 'Oh no.

'You said: Be authentic.
We are, and that's that!
Tell us when you last saw
A witch with no cat.'

Frances Nagle

So Dark

It was so dark
  I couldn't see my hand
in front of my face.
  I thought:
How do I know it's there?
Maybe there's just air
  Where my hand should be.
So I put my hand up
In the dark
To touch my face
Raised my hand to the place
It should be

And it wasn't there.

Trevor Millum

The Invisible Man

The Invisible man is a joker
Who wears an invisible grin
And the usual kind of visible clothes
Which cover up most of him.

But there's nothing above his collar
Or at the end of his sleeves,
And his laughter is like the invisible wind
Which rustles the visible leaves.

When the visible storm clouds gather
He strides through the visible rain
In a special invisible see-through cloak
Then invisibly back again.

But he wears a thick, visible overcoat
To go out when it visibly snows
And the usual visible footprints
Get left wherever he goes.

In the visible heat-haze of summer
And the glare of the visible sun,
He undoes his visible buttons
With invisible fingers and thumb

Takes off his visible jacket,
Looses his visible tie,
Then snaps his visible braces
As he winks an invisible eye.

Last thing in his visible nightgown
Tucked up in his visible bed
He rests on a visible pillow
His weary invisible head

And ponders by visible moonlight
What invisibility means
Then drifts into silent invisible sleep
Full of wonderful visible dreams.

John Mole

Let There Be Light
(Hallumination)

Let there be sunshine
Holy and white
Let there be goodness
Let there be light

Let there be candles
Flickering bright
Torches and lasers
Let there be light

Banish the darkness
Flood out the night
Let there be stars
Let there be light

Let monsters and shadows
Fade out of sight
Let it be dazzling
Let there be light

Goodbye to all things
That give us a fright
Hello to laughter
Let there be light

Let there be happiness
Let there be fun
Let there be something
For everyone

So come on and join in
Our new celebration
Hallo to All Hallows
. . . Hallumination

Paul Cookson

Instructions for the Last Day in October

Leave the cottage at dusk.
Proceed to the sheep's skull
rammed on the gatepost.
Then plod the sodden field
where mists have gathered
to connive like shawled hags.
Now enter the indigo wood.
Above, rooks will be cawing-in
the coming night.
Note the tree's last leaves
hanging like withered hearts.
At the deep ditch's cauldron
crouch and feel the woodland cringe
in the grip of thistles.
Watch, watch spellbound
as bubbles rise from the oily ooze
and know that you have arrived
    at
    Halloween.

Wes Magee

We All Have To Go

The sound drew nearer;
a wheezy, hoarse breathing
as if some heavy weight
were being dragged along.
There was a smell of burnt bones.
A horny, hairy finger edged
round the trickling, slimy wall.
Then a large warty nose,
topped by bloodshot watery eyes,
slowly emerged from the gloom.
The eyes widened, glowing
to a bright red.
Its pace quickened and soon
it towered above us.
The huge slavering mouth opened –
'Any of you lot know where
the toilet is?'

John C. Desmond

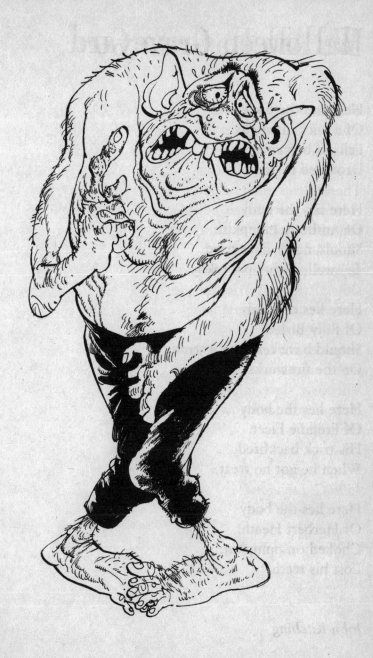

Halloween Graveyard

Here lies the body
Of a wicked witch:
Fell off broomstick;
Drowned in ditch.

Here lies the body
Of Anthony Lumpkin:
Should never have tried
To swallow that pumpkin.

Here lies the body
Of Billy Birks:
Should have read the warning
On the fireworks!

Here lies the body
Of Freddie Fleet.
His trick backfired
When he got no treat.

Here lies the body
Of Herbert Heath:
Choked on pumpkin;
Lost his teeth.

John Kitching

Halloween

Darren's got a pumpkin
Hollowed out a treat
He put it in the window
It scared half the street

I wish I had a pumpkin
But I've not and it's a shame
I've got a scary carrot
But it's not the same.

Roger Stevens

Mask

Wow! What a mask for Halloween,
You really do look horrid –
A big hook nose and pointy chin
And warts upon your forehead!

It's such a realistic mask
And fits you very snugly –
What's that? You haven't got one on?!
Oh boy, you're really ugly!

Colin West

Two Witches Discuss Good Grooming

'How do you keep your teeth so green
Whilst mine remain quite white?
Although I rub them vigorously
With cold slime every night.

'Your eyes are such a lovely shade
Of bloodshot, streaked with puce.
I prod mine daily with a stick
But it isn't any use.

'I envy so the spots and boils
That brighten your complexion
Even rat spit on my face
Left no trace of infection.

'I've even failed to have bad breath
After eating sewage raw,
Yet your halitosis
Can strip paint from a door.'

'My dear, there is no secret,
Now I don't mean to brag.
What you see is nature's work,
I'm just a natural hag.'

John Coldwell

Trick or Treat Riddle

My first letter's in werewolves,
hear their fearsome call?
My second letter is in treat,
but in trick not at all.
My third is found in monster
and it's in Martian too;
my fourth occurs in pumpkin
(not once – there are two).
My fifth's always in witches,
but never found in warlock;
my sixth letter's in Martian
and in monster too.
                    Knock, knock.
My last letter is located
twice in Halloween.

Trick or treat my riddle,
your neck knows when I've been!

Mike Johnson

A Halloween Charm for Sweet Dreams

May the Ghost
   lie in its grave.
May the Vampire
   see the light.
May the Witch
   keep to her cave,
and the Spectre
   melt from sight.

May the Wraith
   stay in the wood.
May the Banshee
   give no fright.
May the Ghoul
   be gone for good,
and the Zombie
   haste its flight.

May the Troll
    no more be seen.
May the Werewolf
    lose its bite.
May all the Spooks
    and Children Green
fade forever
    in
        the
            night . . .

Wes Magee

Monster Manners

The mummy monster told her toddler,
'Remember your etiquette, dear –
Never speak with a mouthful of people,
It's really bad manners I fear . . .'

Clive Webster

What Else?

Dracula sat in the local cafe
And ordered a coffee to drink.
The waiter asked him
'Which kind, sir?' –
'De-coffinated, what do you think . . . ?'

Clive Webster

Halloween Hotpot

Blackhead of a greasy skin
in the cauldron simmering,
hair of nose and wax of ear,
scurf of scalp and salt of tear,
sticky eye and fur of tongue,
plaque of tooth and blood of gum.
For a spell stir at the double,
bring it to the boil
and bubble.

Gina Douthwaite

Bloip!
Bloop!

At the Halloween Party

At the Halloween party
the cake was iced black
and people had cloaks
made from big plastic sacks,
people had fangs
of luminous plastic
and horrible masks
held on with elastic.
There were witches and wizards
and ghosts dressed in sheets.
Pumpkins glowed eerily,
big, fat and round,
apples were bobbed
and some kids nearly drowned,
a magician arrived
and took eggs out of ears
and made Old Uncle Charlie's
false teeth disappear.
A real ghost arrived
but left in a huff
when they told it its costume
was not good enough.
The room decorations
were broomsticks and bats,
skeletons (dangling),
and plasticine cats.

There was screaming and shrieking
and horrible frights
and still, to look forward to,
Fireworks Night.

Marian Swinger

Favourite Book Titles
To Be Found in
the Monster Book Shop

FEE! FI!
FO! FUM!
and Other
Monster Rhymes
by
I. B. A. Giant

The
Vampire
Who Needed
Glasses
by
Mr Neck

A WEREWOLF
JUST LEFT US
FOR DEAD
by
Vic Timm-Speekes

The
Bogeyman
Is Out
Tonight
by
R. U. A. Frade

Richard Caley

We Are Not Alone

When the floorboards creak and hinges squeak
When the TV's off but seems to speak
When the moon is full and you hear a shriek
We are not alone.

When the spiders gather beneath your bed
When they colonize the garden shed
When they spin their webs right above your head
We are not alone.

When the lights are out and there's no one home
When you're by yourself and you're on your own
When the radiators bubble and groan
We are not alone.

When the shadows lengthen round your wall
When you hear deep breathing in the hall
When you think there's no one there at all
We are not alone.

When the branches tap on your windowpane
When the finger twigs scritch scratch again
When something's changed but it looks the same
We are not alone.

When the wallpaper is full of eyes
When the toys in the dark all change in size
When anything's a monster in disguise
We are not alone.

You'd better watch out whatever you do
There's something out there looking at you
When you think you are on your own
We are not
We are not
We are not alone.

Paul Cookson

I'm Right Here

I'm the dream
You didn't want to have
The nightmare driving you mad.

I'm the monster
In the bushes in the park
The footsteps ringing after dark.

I'm the vampire
Flapping round your room
The darkness, shadow and gloom.

I'm the Nasty
The Horrid and Spite
The hairy scary feeling in the night.

I'm the reeking, speaking, stomach-tweaking
Staircase creaking whilst you're sleeping
Creeping so your heart is leaping
Thing.

I'll sing
My werewolf song
Bring along my friend King Kong.

My bones
Will rattle your ears
My moans and groans will stir your fears.

What's that?
Well they are mine
Those tingling fingers down your spine.

Don't scream
Don't make a sound
I'm right here, don't turn around.

David Harmer

Rained Off

The wind's blown out the candle
of my glowing pumpkin head
and I forgot to bring my broomstick,
it's still standing in the shed.

The rain's ruined my paper hat,
it's in tatters at my feet
and I didn't get a single thing
from anyone in my street.

The make-up's all run down my face
I must look a sorry sight
I think I'll give up on Halloween
and wait for Bonfire Night.

Damian Harvey

Building a Bonfire from the Bottom Up

End.

Light.

Add the guy.

Build it higher.

Raid the tip for stuff.

Keep looking for stuff.

Penny for the guy, please missus.

Pray it doesn't rain the week before.

Dry leaves are good if you can find them.

You'll need to beg some spuds from your mams.

Nick from other bommies if you have to. Guard your own.

Next cadge loads of newspapers and old wood from anyone you can.

Start: with a good piece of earthy ground well away from buildings and trees.

Angela Topping

Firework Night

Bonfires blazing
children gazing
fireworks flashing
people dashing
colours fantastic
jumps gymnastic
planet-chasing
rocket-racing
faces glowing
crowds all growing:
stars in flight
this firework night.

Andrew Collett

The Bonfire Potato

The forgotten bonfire potato
In its warm silver nest
Listens to the rocket's raucous launch
Remains silent for the pompous performance
Of the Roman Candle
Keeps quiet as the Glittering Cascade
Has its glamorous few seconds.
Polite and patiently permitting
Every firework in the box
Their moments of blazing glory.

When the final hiss fizzles to silence
Potato
Lets go
Exploding in a splitting,
Spitting, splash,
Streaming starch.

And earns the longest 'OOOOOOOOOOOH!' of the
    evening.

John Coldwell

Firework Night

Firework night! Excitement grows!
  Milk bottles holding rockets
Are lined up on our patios
  As we, with hands in pockets,

Peer through the gloomy mist and fog
  To see what Dad is doing.
Beneath the bed you'll find the dog –
  He knows that something's brewing!

Dad hammers Catherine wheels to trees
  While Roman Candles sizzle.
His match goes out in a passing breeze,
  And now it starts to drizzle!

Mount Etna on the tabletop
  Sends out grey snakes of lava.
Squibs jerk around and make us hop!
  Dad wears his balaclava

To keep the rain off his bald patch.
  'Dad, can you light the bonfire?'
'Oh, all right, then!' He lights a match
  And soon the guy is on fire.

At last the rockets leave their pads
    And split the night-sky, screaming,
Exploding when they reach the top
    With all their colours streaming.

Dad picks up all the empty jars,
    Our sparklers are ignited.
We write our names in silver stars
    And run around, excited.

Then Mother says, 'That's quite enough
    Of all your noisy rackets!
I've cooked you sausages and beans
    And 'tatoes in their jackets.'

So ends another Guy Fawkes' Night:
    The fireworks now are over,
And when we're all sent up to bed
    We go and comfort Rover.

Pam Gidney

Bonfire Night

Fireworks blossom on
The black sugar-paper sky.

The spicy smell of first frost
Makes nostrils tingle.

The bonfire burns like a furnace.
My face is as hot as an iron.

My fleece jacket is snuggled
Around me to keep me warm.

I write my name in air
With my white-hot sparkler.

Before bed, there's hot chocolate,
Floating cushions of marshmallow.

Angela Topping

November 6th – Last Night's Life

Last night's magic, last night's colours,
Last night's sparkle, last night's fizz,
Last night's snap, last night's crackle,
Last night's pop, last night's whizz.

Last night's boom, last night's crash,
Last night's bangs today are found
Blackened, ash stained, shattered cardboard
Dead and scattered on the ground.

Paul Cookson

Remember

as we sit
and watch the embers
we remember
the weeks it took
to build the bommie
scaling walls
and stripping empty houses
then up and down the street
knocking on every door
to ask for wood
or furniture
the old armchairs with broken backs
or the wardrobe that's collapsed

the weeks it took
collecting all those
pennies for the guy
pushing the busted baby buggy
with the lopsided stuffed-sock head
and tied-at-the-bottom kecks
up and down the precinct
begging 'penny for the guy
eh mate?
penny for the guy'

as we sit and watch
the embers
we remember
the night we raided
Jacko's bommie
and the night they raided ours –
broken tables
and a smashed-up chest of drawers
passed hand to hand
over fences
along the walls

then all today
we stayed off school
dragging the wood out
from its last secret hideout
and stacking it up
piling it up
till the top of it touched the sky

then it's like
all those weeks were over
in one sudden blinding flash
from the first match
that lit the kindling sticks
and the ripped-up papers round the bottom

lit the first fuse
for the bangers and the rockets
a flash of burgers and baked potatoes
half cooked in the dying embers
that we rake with glowing sticks now
as we chew the smoky toffee
and remember

Dave Ward

Guy Fawkes' Grin

'Where's my teeth?' moaned Grandad
as Gran moaned, 'Not again.
I hope the dog's not had 'em.
You grandad is a pain.'

Meanwhile, outside Tesco's,
a Guy Fawkes, big and fat,
sat beside my brother
who was holding out a hat.

People said admiringly
as they tossed the money in,
'What a lovely Guy Fawkes
and what a toothy grin!'

Marian Swinger

POEMS CHOSEN BY BRIAN MOSES

SPOOKY SCHOOLS

Prepare to shiver and shake!

A spooktacular collection of poems featuring petrifying playgrounds, skeleton staff and terrifying teachers.

Includes poems by some of the best contemporary poets around.

Be warned: these poems will scare you silly!

The Ghoul Inspectre's Coming

The Ghoul
Inspectre's coming,
dust off your lazy bones –
tidy out your coffins,
polish up your mournful moans.

Liz Brownlee

FIRE-BREATHING POEMS
BY NICK TOCZEK

DRAGONS!

Be dazzled by all things dragon!

A wonderful collection by dragon connoisseur, poet and magician Nick Toczek.

A lively, funny book packed with poems that are perfect to read aloud.

The Magic of Dragons

Her pyrotechnics never fail.
She breathes on things. They burn, but they'll
Return unburned in just two ticks.
Dragon's doing magic tricks.

POEMS BY PAUL COOKSON

A fantastic collection from a well-known and much-loved poet.

From the scintillatingly silly to the thoroughly thoughtful via wicked wordplay, prepare to be delighted and surprised!

A Sumo Wrestler Chappy

A sumo wrestler chappy
One day in the ring was unhappy
When thrown to the ground
His mum pinned him down
And in view of the crowd changed his nappy.

POEMS BY PETER DIXON

THE TORTOISE HAD A MIGHTY ROAR

Step into the amazing world of Peter Dixon!

Read about the important things in life, such as fairy pic-
nics, what animals sounded like before they all swapped
voices, a spider called Big Billy, what Stone-Age school
was like and what goes on in the magic superstore.

from *Before the Days of Noah*

Before the days of Noah
before he built his ark
seagulls sang like nightingales
and lions sang like larks.
The tortoise had a mighty roar
the cockerel had a moo
kitten always eeyored
and elephants just mewed.

A selected list of titles available from Macmillan Children's Books

Spooky Schools
Poems chosen by Brian Moses   0 330 41358 9   £3.99

Dragons!
Fire-breathing poems by Nick Toczek   0 33043744 5   £4.99

Pants on Fire
Poems by Paul Cookson   0 330 41798 3   £3.99

Give us a Goal
Football poems by Paul Cookson   0 330 43654 6   £3.99

The Tortoise Had a Mighty Roar
Poems by Peter Dixon   0 330 41799 1   £4.99